MONSTER BUDDIES

I'M UNDEAD AND HUNGRY!

MEET A ZOMBIE

Shannon Knudsen

illustrated by Chiara Buccheri

MILLBROOK PRESS • MINNEAPOLIS

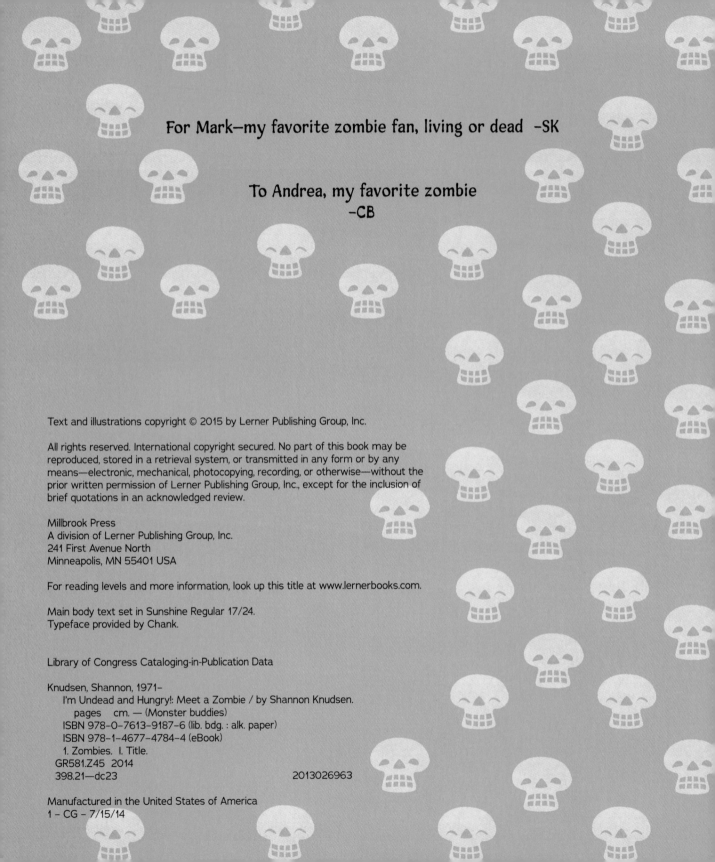

For Mark—my favorite zombie fan, living or dead —SK

To Andrea, my favorite zombie
—CB

Millbrook Press
A division of Lerner Publishing Group, Inc.
241 First Avenue North
Minneapolis, MN 55401 USA

For reading levels and more information, look up this title at www.lernerbooks.com.

Main body text set in Sunshine Regular 17/24.
Typeface provided by Chank.

Library of Congress Cataloging-in-Publication Data

Knudsen, Shannon, 1971–
    I'm Undead and Hungry!: Meet a Zombie / by Shannon Knudsen.
      pages   cm. — (Monster buddies)
    ISBN 978-0-7613-9187-6 (lib. bdg. : alk. paper)
    ISBN 978-1-4677-4784-4 (eBook)
    1. Zombies. I. Title.
  GR581.Z45 2014
  398.21—dc23   2013026963

Manufactured in the United States of America
1 – CG – 7/15/14

TABLE of CONTENTS

Meet a Zombie

I moan for food. I lurch through the streets.
I have nasty gray skin. What am I?
I'm a zombie!
My name's Roscoe, by the way.

What's a zombie? A zombie is a dead person whose body comes back to life. That's right! I'm dead. And I'm alive. How cool is that?

The Truth about Zombies

Getting spooked? Well, you won't run into zombies in real life. You'll meet us in stories and in movies. We're even on TV. But you won't find us in your neighborhood. Probably.

What makes a zombie a zombie? Well, all zombies start as people. Then something goes wrong. I caught a nasty virus. I died, but I didn't stay dead for long. I hopped out of my grave and went for a walk. It sure felt good to stretch my legs!

There are other ways to become a zombie. Some crazy scientists brought my friend Mia back to life. Surprise!

She escaped from their lab.

BRAINS

TRASH

BONES

Hungry and Tough

Zombies are always looking for their next meal. I'm not picky about what I eat. My favorite food is people, but I snack on all kinds of animals. Some zombies won't eat anything but human brains, though. Mmm, mmm . . .

You might think a brain-eating monster would be smart.
Guess again! Most zombies can't think. We can't even talk.

We just moan and groan.

What's a zombie good at besides eating? Making more zombies! If a zombie bites you, watch out. You might become one of us.

Don't say I didn't warn you!

The best thing about being a zombie is that we're tough. We don't feel pain at all. But sometimes fire will keep us away.

Don't tell my friends I told you!

Worried a zombie is after you? You can always take off running. Zombies are stiff and slow. If a bunch of monsters had a race, you can bet the zombies would lose.

We're clumsy too. Once I tried to take dance lessons. I wanted to become more graceful. But no one would dance with me. Everyone thought I would take a bite out of my partner!

Zombies Everywhere

You can find zombies all over the world. Folks from many countries have told tales about the dead returning to life. These stories have spooked people for hundreds of years.

In Haiti, some people practice a religion called voodoo.
In some voodoo stories, magic wakes up the dead.

China has its own zombies. They're so stiff that they can't walk. They have to hop to get around! If you meet a Chinese zombie, hold up a mirror. They are scared of their own faces!

Old stories from northern Europe tell about a different kind of zombie. Norse zombies live in their graves. Sounds pretty chilly to me. But these zombies have treasure to guard.

Don't even think about stealing it!

Beware of the Zombies!

Now you know the deal about zombies. It's a good thing we aren't real, right? After all, no one wants to be a zombie snack.

Hey, I'm feeling a little hungry. Could you come closer? Closer . . . closer . . .

CHOMP!

A Zombie's Day Writing Activity

You've learned a lot about zombies. Now it's time to show off your zombie brains! Grab a pencil and a piece of paper. Write a short story about what a zombie's day is like. Does it go to school? Does it hang out with other zombies? What does it do for fun? Draw a picture to go with your story.

GLOSSARY

death: the end of life

grave: a space in the ground where a dead body is buried

lab: a place where scientists do their work

Norse: from Norway or Scandinavia

virus: a tiny living thing that lives inside other living things and makes them sick

voodoo: a religion in Haiti. Many parts of voodoo come from West Africa.

zombie: a dead person who comes back to life

TO LEARN MORE

Books

Crow, Krysten. *Zombelina.* New York: Walker Books for Young Readers, 2013.
Zombelina is about to dance her first ballet. Will stage fright ruin her big night?

DiPucchio, Kelly. *Zombie in Love.* New York: Atheneum Books for Young Readers, 2011.
Join Mortimer the zombie on his first date in this silly picture book.

Website

PBS Kids: Happy Halloween
http://pbskids.org/halloween
In the mood for something spooky? Visit this website for fun, Halloween-themed activities.

INDEX